Dear Parent:
Your child's love of reading starts here!

Every child learns to read in a different way and at his or her own speed. Some go back and forth between reading levels and read favorite books again and again. Others read through each level in order. You can help your young reader improve and become more confident by encouraging his or her own interests and abilities. From books your child reads with you to the first books he or she reads alone, there are I Can Read Books for every stage of reading:

My First **SHARED READING**
Basic language, word repetition, and whimsical illustrations, ideal for sharing with your emergent reader

1 **BEGINNING READING**
Short sentences, familiar words, and simple concepts for children eager to read on their own

2 **READING WITH HELP**
Engaging stories, longer sentences, and language play for developing readers

3 **READING ALONE**
Complex plots, challenging vocabulary, and high-interest topics for the independent reader

4 **ADVANCED READING**
Short paragraphs, chapters, and exciting themes for the perfect bridge to chapter books

I Can Read Books have introduced children to the joy of reading since 1957. Featuring award-winning authors and illustrators and a fabulous cast of beloved characters, I Can Read Books set the standard for beginning readers.

A lifetime of discovery begins with the magical words **"I Can Read!"**

Visit www.icanread.com for information on enriching your child's reading experience.

I Can Read Book® is a trademark of HarperCollins Publishers.

Superman: Bizarro's Last Laugh
Copyright © 2017 DC Comics.
SUPERMAN and all related characters and elements © & ™ DC Comics.
(s17)

HARP36465
Manufactured in U.S.A. No part of this book may be used or reproduced in any manner whatsoever without written
permission except in the case of brief quotations embodied in critical articles and reviews. For information address
HarperCollins Children's Books, a division of HarperCollins Publishers, 195 Broadway, New York, NY 10007.
www.harpercollinschildrens.com

Library of Congress Control Number: 2016939550
ISBN 978-0-06-236089-2

Book design by Erica De Chavez

17 18 19 20 21 LSCC 10 9 8 7 6 5 4 3 2
❖
First Edition

SUPERMAN

BIZARRO'S LAST LAUGH

by Donald Lemke

pictures by Patrick Spaziante

Superman created by Jerry Siegel and Joe Shuster

By special arrangement with the Jerry Siegel family

HARPER

An Imprint of HarperCollinsPublishers

CLARK KENT

Clark Kent is a reporter at the *Daily Planet* newspaper. He is secretly Superman.

SUPERMAN

Superman, also known as the Man of Steel, has many amazing superpowers, including heat vision and freeze breath.

LOIS LANE

Lois Lane is a reporter at the *Daily Planet* newspaper. She works with Clark Kent.

SUPERGIRL

Supergirl is Superman's heroic teenage cousin. She has the same superpowers as the Man of Steel.

THE *DAILY* PLANET

The *Daily Planet* is the largest newspaper in the city of Metropolis.

BIZARRO

Bizarro is from Bizarro World, where everything is the opposite of Earth. His superpowers are the opposite of Superman's powers.

Inside the Daily Planet Building, reporter Clark Kent groaned. His coworkers laughed nearby. Clark could not concentrate.

"What's all the noise?" Clark asked.

Fellow reporter Lois Lane pointed

at a video on her computer screen.

A truck sped toward a man.

Suddenly, a blue-and-red streak

appeared in the sky—Superman!

The super hero flew down.

He lifted the truck

before it hit the man.

Then soupy concrete spilled

all over the hero.

Everyone laughed.

"Why on earth would anyone

find that funny?" Clark said.

A strange being

watched the same video

from a square-shaped planet.

Bizarro World was light-years away.

Everything there

was the opposite of Earth,

including its worst hero, Bizarro.

"Superman finally do

something wrong," Bizarro said.

He jumped into his rocket ship.

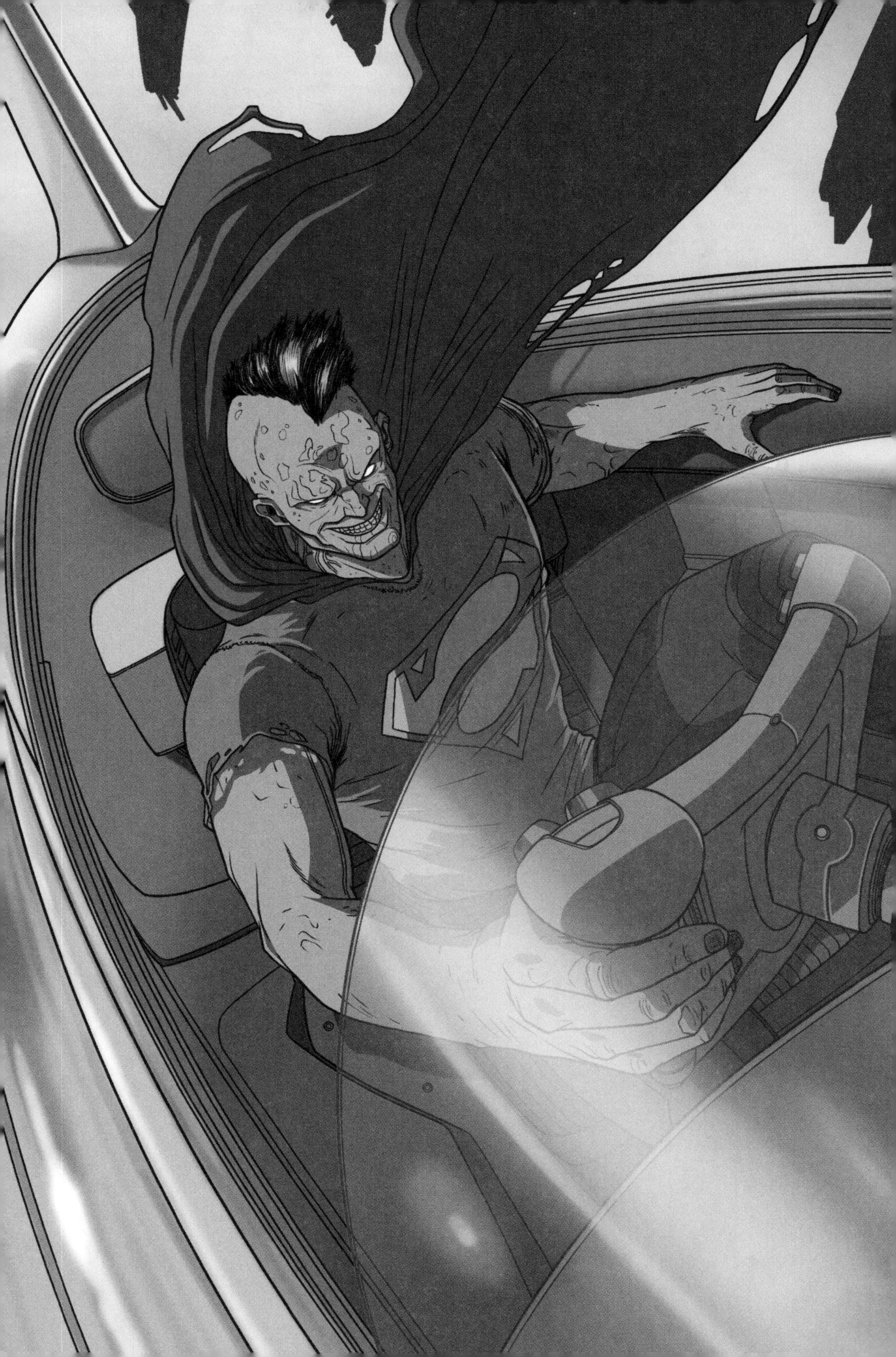

A few days later, Bizarro crashed down in Metropolis. People screamed and ran away.

Clark heard the screams.
He ducked into a nearby closet
and shed his glasses, suit, and tie,
revealing a blue-and-red suit.
He was Superman!

The Man of Steel arrived downtown.

Bizarro flew above him.

He held a giant garbage truck.

"Me help make clean city

big mess!" Bizarro shouted.

He shook the truck.

Pizza boxes, old food,

and other garbage rained down.

Superman blasted the trash

with his heat vision!

The trash turned to dust.

Soon the streets were covered.

A teenager giggled.

Superman turned and saw

his cousin, Supergirl.

"Looks like someone wants

to play dirty," she joked.

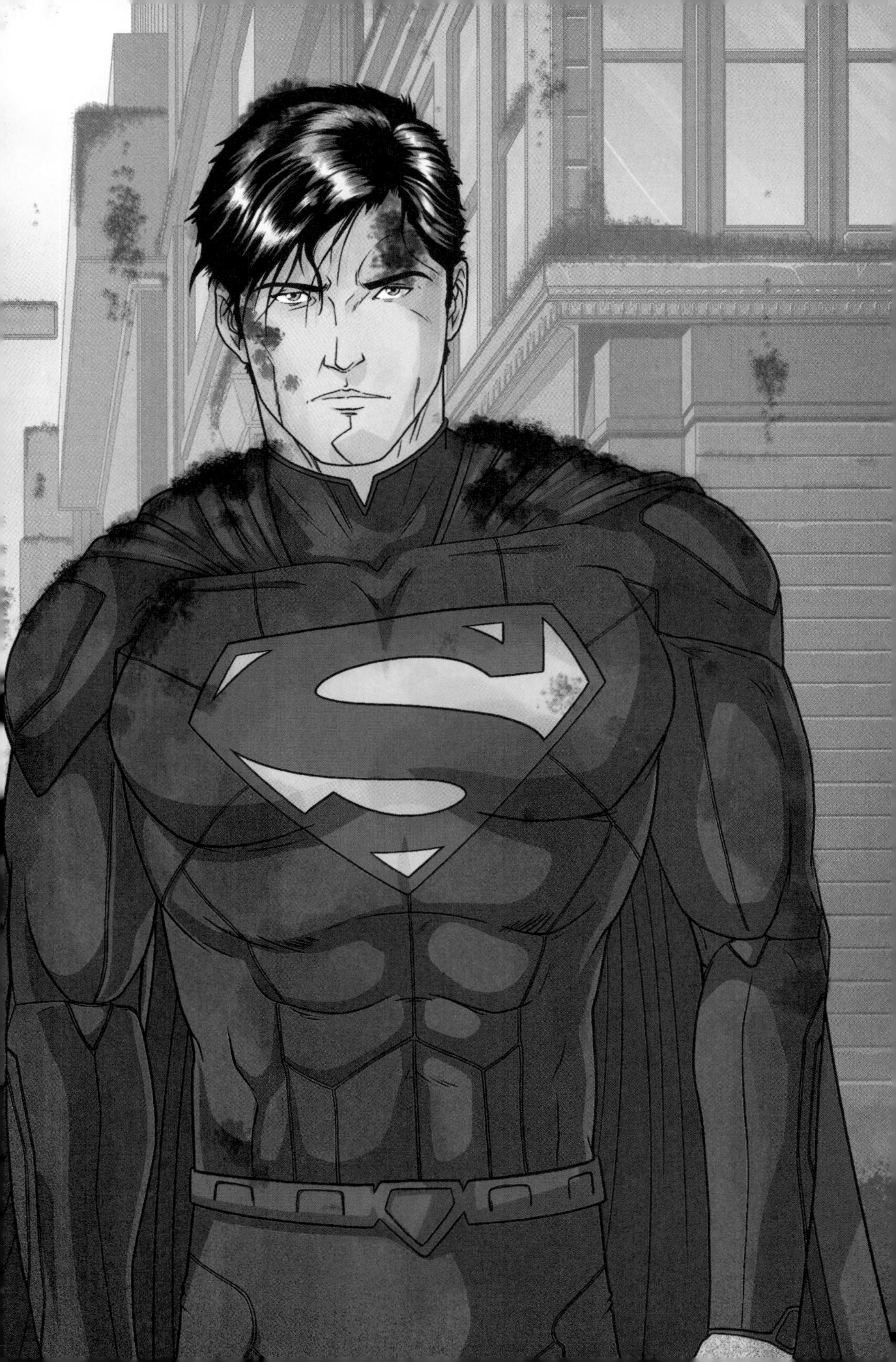

Bizarro threw the garbage truck at Supergirl.

"Time to take out the trash!" she said.

She punched the truck.

Garbage spilled over Supergirl,

covering her in a sticky mess.

"Yuck!" she said.

"One person's trash is another

person's treasure," Superman joked.

Bizarro watched the angry duo.

"Me make heroes happy!" he said.

"Me do more."

Bizarro swooped down.

He froze fire hydrants

with his freeze vision.

The icy hydrants cracked.

Water spurted into the air.

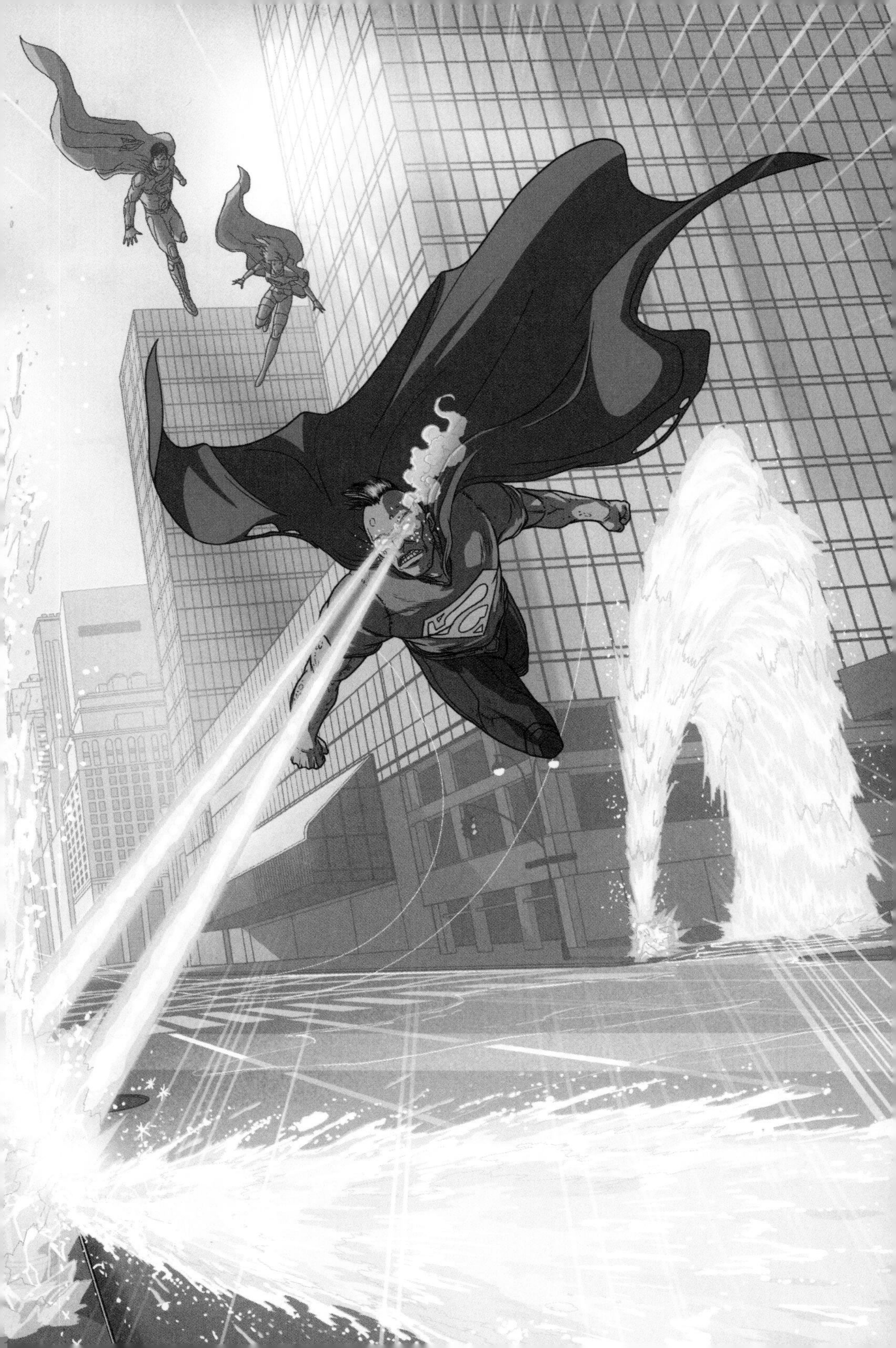

Water flooded the streets.

"What do we do?" Supergirl asked.

"Simple," Superman said.

"We fight fire with fire!"

The super heroes filled
their lungs with air. *Whoosh!*
They blasted the flooded streets
with their freeze breath.

The water froze quickly.

Bizarro tried to move

but he was stuck in solid ice.

"Me just warming up!" he cried.

People returned to the streets.

They slid across the ice

like Olympic skaters.

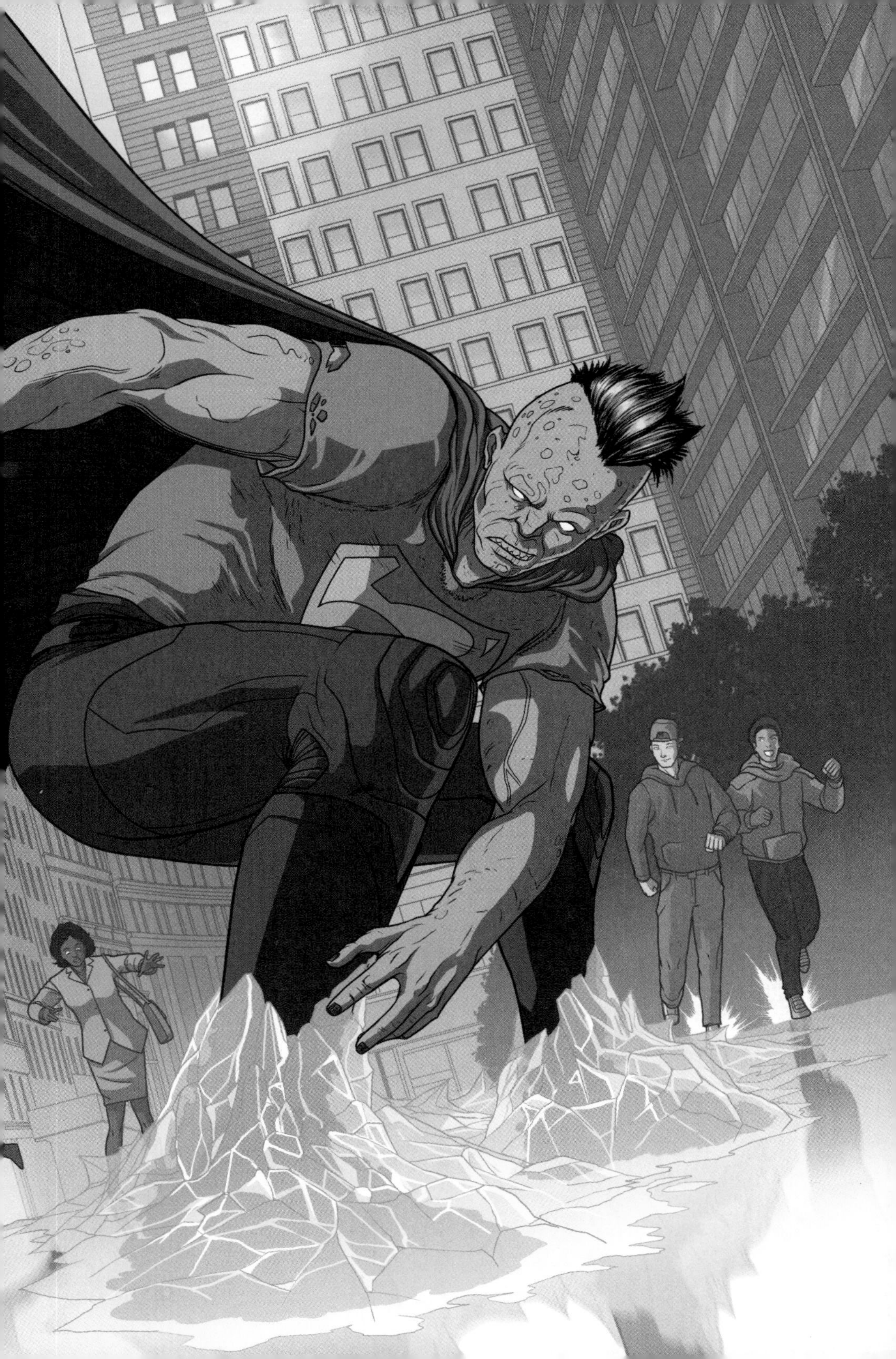

Some people slipped and fell.

They laughed at themselves

and at each other.

The super heroes joined the fun.

Bizarro was confused
by the happy people and heroes.
"Why they laugh?"
he said.

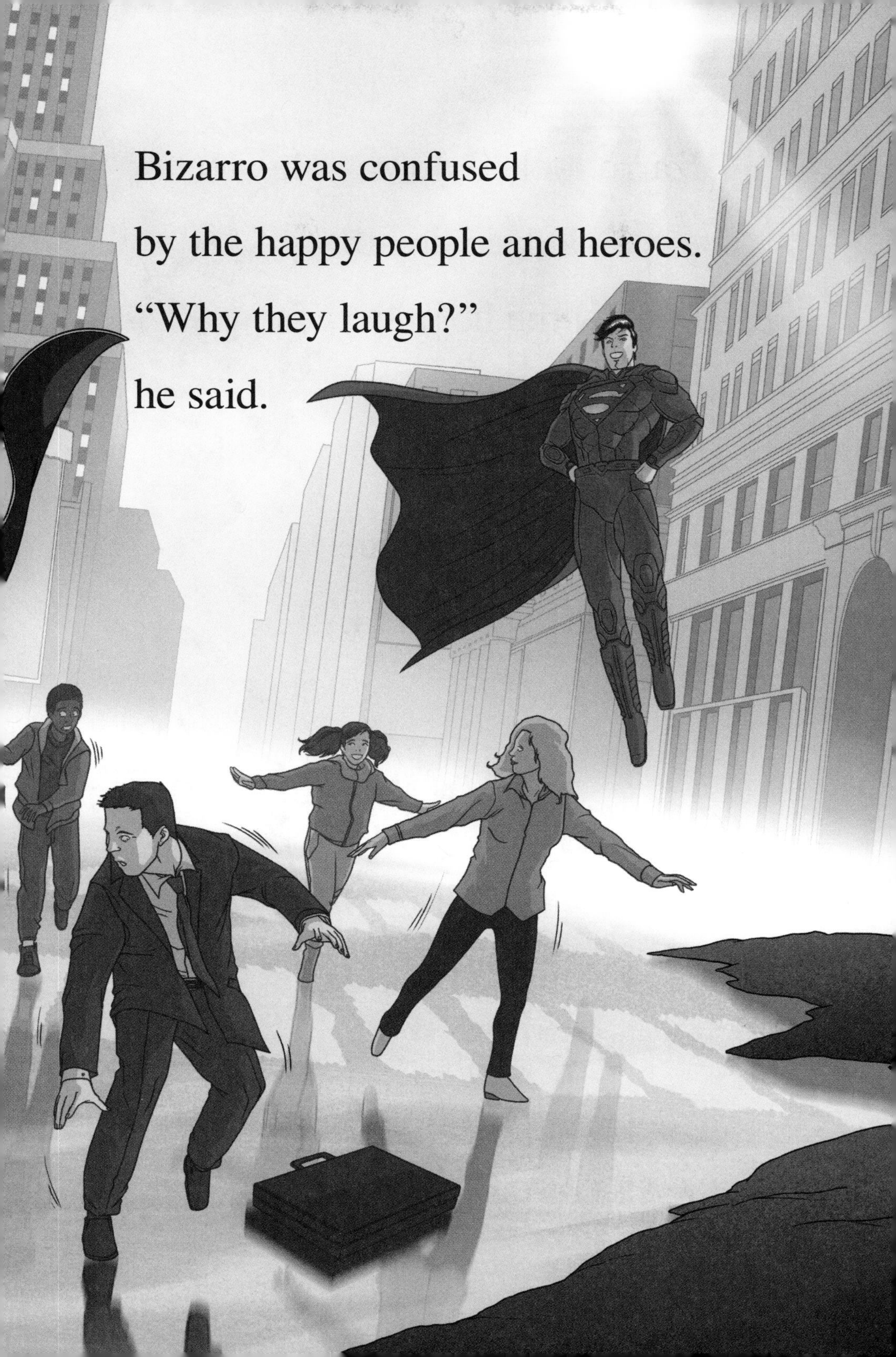

Bizarro looked down at his feet.
He took a deep breath
and blew the hot air
out quickly.
Fwoosh!
Bizarro melted the ice
with his flame breath.
He was free!

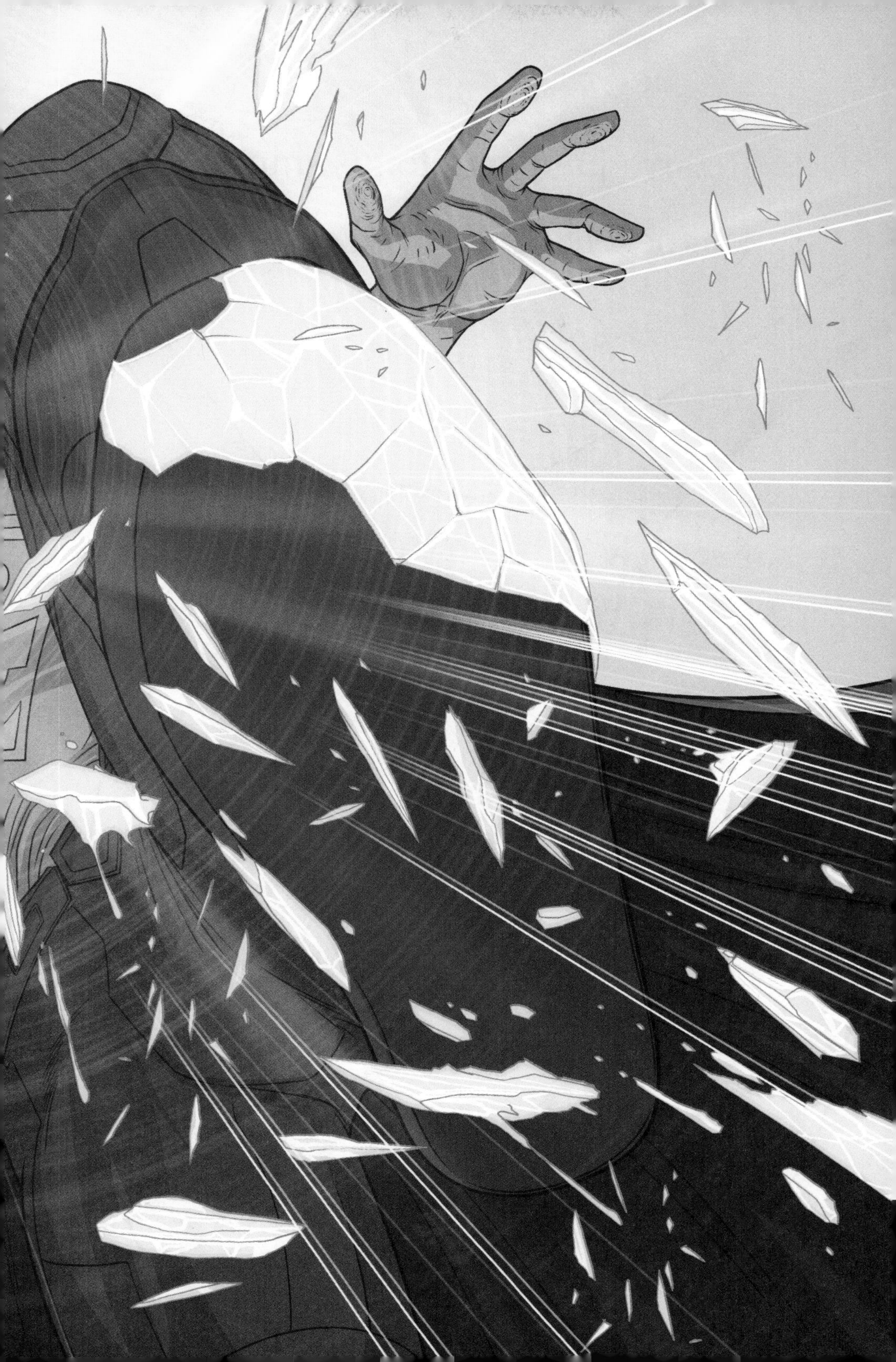

Bizarro jumped into his ship.

He rocketed back to Bizarro World.

When the ice melted,

the water cleared

most of the ash and the trash

from the city streets.

The heroes cleaned up the rest.

"Well, that headache is gone," said Superman.

"Yep," Supergirl agreed.

"I guess laughter really is the best medicine."